RiO

THE JUNIOR NOVEL

HarperFestival is an imprint of HarperCollins Publishers.
Rio: The Junior Novel
Rio © 2010 Twentieth Century Fox Film Corporation. All rights reserved.
Printed in the United States of America.

Library of Congress catalog card number: 2010928925
ISBN 978-0-06-202269-1
Typography by Rick Farley
11 12 13 14 15   LP/CW   10 9 8 7 6 5 4 3
❖
First Edition

RiO

THE JUNIOR NOVEL

Adapted by Lexa Hillyer
Based on the motion picture screenplay by
Todd R. Jones and Earl Richey Jones

An Imprint of HarperCollinsPublishers

Rio

THE JUNIOR NOVEL

In the beginning...

The mist began to melt away as the sun rose over the lush green canopy of trees.

A faint whistle could be heard as a single bird swooped down from a branch, calling to the other birds beneath him. With that one whistle, all the other birds in the jungle began to respond. Pretty soon, the entire Brazilian rain forest was full of the sounds of birds singing. Even a couple of little eggs cracked open in a nest, and two newborn chicks popped out to dance!

"Hey!" a mother bird shouted as a big group

1

of colorful parrots and toucans and cockatiels flew by. But none of them slowed down—the rain forest was hopping with samba-style music and all the birds were excited to start the new day.

All except one.

Little baby Blu sat alone in his nest, frozen with fear. He was a very young bird—only just hatched—and he didn't yet know how to fly! He desperately wanted to join the others in their song and dance, but he was too afraid. The nest seemed to be *very* high up and just looking down made him dizzy.

But then he watched the beautiful birds of all varieties having such a fun time, and something surprising happened. He noticed he was bobbing his head a little to the rhythm. Pretty soon, he was tapping his talons, getting into the groove!

All of a sudden, Blu got scared again—it seemed like his whole nest was vibrating! But when he turned around, he realized what was causing all the vibrations: his own butt! He was shaking his tail feathers to the music!

Just then a mother and her new chicks

soared past his nest and Blu felt a surge of inspiration—now was the time!

He took one timid step toward the edge of his nest. Then another. And then . . . just as Blu was about to take the plunge out of his nest and into the beautiful dancing canopy of birds and leaves below, he heard an ugly, rumbling, roaring noise. The birds stopped singing all at once and as Blu watched, he saw something he'd never seen before. Something hulking and square and . . .

It was a truck. One of many trucks and jeeps full of poachers—men who steal wild birds! All the birds darted this way and that in a panic. The men tossed nets through the air as birds of all shapes and sizes squawked with fear.

Blu turned his head in either direction, watching as the birds who one minute ago had been singing at the top of their lungs were now caught in the nets. It was a horrible sight. He heard a loud sound and got startled. As he jumped out of the way, he hit the edge of his nest . . . and slipped!

Down, down, down Blu was falling! He tried to open his wings and flap them but it was no use—he hadn't learned how to fly yet. Instead, he plopped all the way to the ground, landing in a large pile of leaves. Just as he looked up at his towering nest, a cage dropped down around him.

He had been caught.

The poachers packed Blu's cage into a shipping crate. Then they slammed a door on a cargo plane, which took off down the runway with little Blu inside.

Meanwhile, in a sleepy town in Minnesota called Moose Lake Village, a little girl named Linda was wishing and hoping for the perfect present. Moose Lake Village was cold and quiet and flat. There were no lush green trees or brightly colored birds here. There was snow—and lots of it. Snow blanketed the beautiful countryside as far as the eye could see.

In the morning, as the town was just waking up, a truck containing Blu's cage rumbled along. All of a sudden, as the truck lurched over some snow, one of the locks on the back door shook loose, and out fell the crate—with Blu still inside. The truck turned a corner and was gone, leaving Blu's crate all alone in the street.

Blu chirped and chirped for help, until finally a shadow passed over him. The shadow belonged to Linda. She was smiling as her hands reached inside the crate and picked Blu up. Little Blu was nervous at first, but then he smiled a little, too. He knew he'd be safe and happy with this girl.

And for many years, he was. . . .

CHAPTER

1

Fifteen years later ...

Linda grew up into a kind young woman who owned a bookstore. For the past fifteen years, she had raised Blu. When Linda was eight, she was already giving Blu his medicine all by herself. When she turned ten, she let Blu help her blow out her birthday candles. When she went to the prom, Blu was her date. They had done everything together. The two were the closest of friends.

And this morning was just like any other morning at Linda's house.

It was time to go to work and open up the

bookstore. Inside Linda's bedroom, a loud alarm went off. Linda was sleepy. She hit her alarm clock, mumbling and grumpy, but the alarm just kept going.

Finally Linda realized that it wasn't the alarm clock making that loud, annoying noise. It was Blu! Linda laughed and tapped Blu on the head, pretending he was the alarm clock. Blu picked up Linda's glasses in his beak and dropped them onto her face.

"Good morning, Blu!" Linda said cheerfully.

Then Blu and Linda went about their morning routine, making toast together and pouring Blu's favorite colorful, fruity cereal into his bowl. They ate breakfast together, and then brushed their teeth together, but Blu accidentally swallowed his toothpaste! Blu couldn't help it—he burped.

"Ew!" said Linda. Then she found Blu's vitamins and tried to give them to him, but Blu refused, bending in every possible direction to avoid them. Finally Linda distracted Blu by shaking the cereal box, and Blu opened his mouth. As he did, she shoved in the spoonful of bird vitamins.

Blu leaped through rings and across shelves and slid down the banister and made his way to the door, ready for a long day's work at the bookstore.

When they got to the bookstore, Linda and Blu tidied up the shop. Linda would place a stack of books on the shelf, and then Blu would slide by on the gliding ladder and make sure they were stacked straight. When they finished cleaning up and getting ready, Blu went to flip over the Open sign. He bumped his wing with Linda's fist, and they both smiled.

They loved their life together!

The only thing was they didn't have very many customers in their bookstore. Moose Lake Village was a small town where few people ever came.

Linda and Blu spent the day at the bookstore playing Jenga. The tower of Jenga blocks had gotten very high, and it was just about to be Blu's turn to go, when they heard the store doorbell jingle. Blu got distracted and the Jenga blocks went tumbling down. "I win! I win! I never win!" Linda shouted happily.

But as Linda was shouting, a strange man entered the store.

Linda looked at the man, confused.

"Are you looking for a book?" she asked him.

The man stared her in the eyes. "No. I've come six thousand miles looking for the two of *you.*"

CHAPTER

2

Linda led the strange man into the shop and examined his business card. The card said:

TULIO MONTEIRO
DOCTOR OF ORNITHOLOGY

Linda took a good look at the man—Tulio. He was actually kind of cute.

Tulio slowly approached Blu. "Ooooh, he's magnificent!" Tulio began to flap around, squawking and making funny birdlike motions. "Squaaaawk! Squawk-squawk-squawwwwk!"

Blu tried to understand what Tulio was saying—or squawking—in bird language. It sounded like total nonsense!

"Uhhh, this guy is freaking me out over here!" Blu announced. "Linda? A little help here?" Blu said this in bird language, of course, which sounds to humans like just plain old squawking.

And so Linda thought Blu was actually communicating with Tulio!

"Do you see that?" Linda exclaimed. "You're really talking to each other! Blu understands you!"

Tulio blushed proudly. He cleared his throat to transition from squawking to talking, and then told Linda, "I've been studying their language! I introduced myself and shook my tail feathers counterclockwise, thus deferring to his dominance."

"Really?" Blu muttered to himself. "Because I didn't get that at all."

"But . . . how did you find out about Blu?" Linda asked.

"I saw one of your videos!" Tulio pulled out his smart phone and went online. "Check this out!"

He held up his phone and played one of the videos Linda had made of Blu doing silly tricks for fun.

"The winters here are, uh," she said, laughing nervously, "very long. There's not much else to do for fun. . . ."

Tulio smiled. "His plumage is magnificent." He examined Blu, lifting his wings.

"Careful," said Linda. "He's very delicate. I mean, he doesn't even fly. . . ."

"Impossible!" said Tulio. "He's a perfect specimen!" He picked up Blu.

"Wait, what are you doing?" asked Linda.

"Don't worry, some birds just need a little encouragement. Their natural instincts will take over." Tulio threw Blu into the air, thinking he would start to flap his wings and fly.

But Blu screamed and plummeted straight to the floor!

"Well, almost always . . . ," Tulio muttered.

"Are you okay, Blu?" Linda asked, running over to him.

"I'm so sorry," said Tulio. "I guess I was just excited. I mean, you know your macaw is a very special bird. As far as we know, Blu is the last male of his kind."

Blu, who was listening along to the conversation, gasped. "I'm the *last* of my kind?"

"We recently found a female of this kind," Tulio continued. "We hope to bring them together so they can mate and save their species."

"And how would we do that?" Linda asked.

"It's all set up!" Tulio said. "You just have to bring Blu to Rio de Janeiro!"

"Wait," Linda interrupted. "Rio? As in, Brazil? That's so far away!"

Blu started to worry. "This is crazy!" he squawked. "Rio is like halfway around the world!" He spun a globe around with his wing as he tried to find it.

Linda focused on rearranging some of her books, talking to Tulio over her shoulder. "Nope! No, no, no, no, no. See, Blu and I aren't . . . well, we're not exactly pack-up-and-go-to-Brazil kind of people! And besides . . . we don't like to fly."

Tulio followed Linda through the shop, trying to convince her to change her mind. "Linda," he said, "I promise you, you'll be with

Blu every step of the way. And I will be there with you."

"Yeah." Linda sighed. "It's just . . . I don't know. I'm sorry. It's just that . . . well . . . no. The answer is no."

"Linda, don't you see?" he pleaded. "If Blu were gone, this whole species would be gone. Could you imagine a world without Blu, or any other birds like him? Please. Think about it." He placed his business card on the table and walked out of the shop.

This was the hardest decision Linda had ever had to make. . . .

Later on that night, Blu stood on the top shelf of the bookcase, talking to himself while he scribbled calculations onto a notebook. "Hmm. Natural instincts. Whatever. There's nothing natural about being thrown halfway across the room! Okay, okay. Let's see here. I can figure this out. Just need to crunch some numbers. Aha! I have my angles just right. I've adjusted for wind shear . . . yes, right. Good."

Blu was nervous. He had planned everything just right, but he was still a bit . . . scared.

Flying was no easy task! He continued muttering to himself: "Okay, so I am rested and relaxed. I just need the final safety procedures which should come from . . . uh . . . myself. Yes, so, uh, here they are! You can have them!" Blu was talking to himself, one of his favorite pastimes. "Why, thank you!" he said to himself. "No problem," he replied to himself.

Blu flapped open his wings, getting ready to fly. Now that he was older, his wings had grown a lot. "My flaps are open. Perfect!" He flexed his talons to check his landing gear. Then he fluttered his tail feathers and shook his butt. "Not bad," he said to himself, feeling a bit proud of his tail flaps. It seemed he was ready to go!

He decided to keep it simple, just do one step at a time. "Thrust, lift, drag, weight. Thrust, lift, drag, weight." He repeated these words as he took a running start across the shelf.

But he screeched to a halt at the edge and looked down. As he came to a stop, he lost his balance and tumbled off the shelf, hitting one shelf after another as he fell, before slamming down onto the hard wood floor. Ow!

Blu looked up and saw Linda watching him. He ambled over. It was high time they had a talk.

Blu hopped up on Linda's knee like he'd done a thousand times before. "I promised I would always look out for you," Linda said. "Didn't I?"

Blu just stared back at her.

She went on. "Have I ever broken a promise? I wouldn't do this if it wasn't the right thing to do. So, what do you say, Blu? Rio?" She held out her fist toward him.

He bumped her fist with his head and then they did their special handshake.

"That's my big, brave boy," Linda said, grinning at last. "Now, let's go. We've got a plane to catch!"

CHAPTER

3

Blu and Linda drove through the bustling city, past beautiful sandy beaches, toward the Conservation Center in Rio de Janeiro. They were excited by all the colors they saw and the music they heard, but Linda still made sure she had sunscreen on her nose and Blu had some on his beak.

A canary and a cardinal flew past and tried to talk to Blu, but they realized quickly from Blu's accent that he was new there—he was a tourist.

"That's funny!" said the canary, whose

name was Nico. "You sure don't *look* like a tourist! But bird, behind bars—that's no way to see Rio! It's the most exciting city in the world!"

The other bird, Pedro, said "Man, you got to get out so you can feel it in your feathers. Stand back, we're gonna pop open your cage!"

"No really," said Blu. "I'm fine."

"Okay. Suit yourself," said Nico.

"Welcome to Rio. *Ciao*," said Pedro.

"Bem vindo," said Nico as he and Pedro flew off.

Blu watched them go. "Yes, yes, bem . . . and to you as well."

Meanwhile, Linda and Tulio sat in the front seat of the jeep, watching the people of Rio dancing by in wild costumes.

"Why are they dressed like that?" Linda asked. "What's going on?"

Tulio replied, "You've arrived in time for Carnavale!"

"Carnavale? What's that?" Linda asked.

"It's the biggest party in the world! A time to cut loose!" Tulio said. Just then a woman in a very skimpy costume danced by.

"Oh my gosh!" Linda said, feeling a bit embarrassed.

But Tulio just smiled and said, "Oh . . . that lady is just my uh, my dentist!" Tulio said as the woman danced by.

The woman looked over her shoulder at Tulio and shouted, "Don't forget to floss!" as she shook her butt and danced away.

Tulio laughed when he saw Linda's face. "If you think that's something, by tomorrow, the party will take over the whole city!"

The jeep finally pulled into the driveway at the Conservation Center.

"So," Tulio said, helping them out of the car. "This is the heart and soul of our aviary— where we keep the birds." He led Linda through a large room inside the Conservation Center. "It is our treatment room." As he spoke, one of the birds flew over to him.

"They must really like you," Linda said.

Just then a bunch of birds shot past her head and landed all over Tulio. He laughed—it was clear that he loved the birds as much as the birds loved him. He fed them straight from his mouth!

"Many of these birds were rescued from smugglers," he said to Linda.

"Smugglers?" she asked.

"Yes. Smugglers steal wild birds and try to sell them. The poor birds are often hurt or even killed in the process. Just look at this poor scared guy here," Tulio said, reaching out to a large white bird—a cockatoo—who looked very sick and very afraid. "Hey, buddy!" Tulio whispered at the bird. "You're looking great today! Much better. Much better."

Tulio stroked the bird's feathers and Linda smiled at the bird.

"So where's Jewel?" Linda asked. Jewel was the name of the female bird they were planning to introduce to Blu. She was the only other bird of his kind.

"Oh, we have a special place for Jewel," Tulio explained. "She is very . . . spirited!"

Tulio walked over to one of the men who worked at the Conservation Center. The man turned, groaning in pain—because huge chunks of his hair were ripped out. And he had scratches on his face. Jewel had attacked the worker! "Spirited," the man muttered, rubbing one of his cuts. "I'll say."

"Jewel did *that*?" Blu squawked, getting nervous all over again. "Okay, I'm gonna go home now."

But Tulio leaned in toward Blu and spoke to him in a calm voice. "Blu," he said, "are you ready to meet your new girlfriend?"

Blu huddled in the back of his cage. No, he certainly did *not* want to meet her!

"Don't worry," Tulio continued. "I'll make you irresistible. She'll love you!"

Tulio spent a long time grooming Blu so that his feathers puffed out beautifully. Then Blu stood in the aviary, waiting to meet Jewel.

The room came alive with a flowing stream and wonderful fake sunlight. But as usual, Blu was a bit nervous . . . to say the least. And then a gorgeous, exotic bird flew into the room. That was Jewel!

Blu thought Jewel was beautiful. The most beautiful bird he had ever seen!

"She's like an angel!" Blu said aloud. "An

angel who is getting really close—aaaagh!"

Jewel had swooped down close to Blu and pinned him to the floor with her sharp talons.

Jewel cocked her head and looked Blu in the eye. "Where did *you* come from?" she asked. "What are you doing here?"

Blu tried to answer her, but she was squishing his neck! "Yddlh sttng nn mmmmch," he muttered.

"What?" asked Jewel.

Blu whispered as loud as he could, "You're standing . . . on my . . . throat!"

Jewel moved away. "Oh, sorry," she said.

Blu got up and tried to act normal. "You know, I need my throat for talking. So, thanks," he said.

"Um, who *are* you?" asked Jewel.

"My name is Blu. You know, like the cheese? With mold on it. That smells really bad." *Ugh,* Blu thought, *stupid! That sounded so stupid!*

"All right," said Jewel, "come on. We don't have much time." She grabbed him by the wing and pulled him toward a tree. Blu hit his head on a branch.

"W-w-w-wait!" said Blu. "Ow!"

"Are you ready?" asked Jewel.

"For what?" Blu was getting more and more nervous. Then it hit him. She wanted to kiss. . . . "Oh," he stuttered. "Um, well, *wow*. Okay. Ummm . . . sure. Why not? No problem. Let's ah . . . let's do this!"

"All right!" said Jewel.

Blu took a deep breath. He closed his eyes tight and tried to prepare himself to kiss Jewel.

"Ew!"

"What?" Blu opened his eyes.

Jewel pushed Blu away.

"But!" said Blu, "I thought you wanted me to . . . but you know, just for . . . wait. What are you trying to do?"

"I'm trying to escape, of course," said Jewel.

Oh! thought Blu. *She doesn't want to kiss. She wants to escape.* Blu was relieved.

"Yeah, uh, escape! That was where I was going with that. That thing I just did . . . "

"Wwwwwait," shouted Jewel. "Did you actually think we were going to *kiss*? Even though we just *met*?!"

"No!" Blu stammered. "No, no, no! It's

not . . . I just . . . that's not what I meant! I mean, I know how my feathers look, but I'm not that kind of bird."

Linda and Tulio, who were watching the two birds' meeting from the observation room, looked at each other in concern. This was not working the way they had planned! Blu was too awkward and Jewel didn't seem interested in him at all. This was supposed to be a bird romance, not a bird fight!

Tulio shrugged and said, "I think they need a little help." Then he turned on some soft music. "This should set the mood!"

But Jewel glared at Blu when she heard the music start playing.

"What?" said Blu. "I had *nothing* to do with the music choice! But um, you have to admit . . . it's actually a pretty good song." Then Blu started to sing along with the music. But Blu's awful singing just made Jewel more upset. She decided to take matters into her own talons and flew quickly at Blu. As she landed on him, hard, the branch he was standing on cracked and began to fall. Jewel landed on top of Blu on the ground.

Blu and Jewel were miserable and annoyed. But to Tulio and Linda, who were watching from afar, it looked like the two birds were hugging!

Linda clapped her hands and raised her eyebrows. "Wow!" she said. "That was fast!"

Tulio smiled. "Lionel Richie song. Works every time. We should probably give these two lovebirds some privacy now."

They headed out of the observation room.

But Linda was still worried. "I'm not so sure I should leave Blu here alone."

"Oh no, no, no," Tulio said smiling, "don't worry. Sylvio will keep an eye on them all night."

Sylvio was a very large, very serious security guard. He could stab a fly with a pencil—that's how fast Sylvio was.

"And besides," Tulio continued as they walked past Sylvio, "Blu's got Jewel to keep him company!"

Little did Linda and Tulio know that by then Jewel and Blu were strangling each other.

"Okay, look!" Blu said, choking. "We got off to a—bad start—but if you let me live—maybe you'll—get to like me. . . ."

Jewel laughed at him. "Ha! Not if you were the last Spix's Macaw on earth!"

Blu rubbed his throat and stared at her. "Don't you know?" he muttered, still trying to catch his breath. "I *am* the last Spix's Macaw on earth."

Jewel stared at Blu in shock.

He stared right back at her and said, "That's why I'm . . . here. To meet you. We're the only ones left."

CHAPTER

Later on that evening, long after Blu and Jewel had stopped fighting and decided to just go to sleep, Sylvio stood guard at the aviary. Sylvio was normally a very serious and tough guard. He was big and strong and good at his job of protecting the birds. But the beat of Carnavale was in the air. He could hear samba music playing everywhere. Sylvio started to wiggle and dance. He pulled off his security guard shirt and underneath it was a bright and very silly-looking Carnavale dance costume!

But just as he was really getting into the

groove, Sylvio heard a loud SMASH. Glass shattered in the Conservation Center. Uh-oh. Could the birds be in danger?

Sylvio dashed over to where the noise came from, and looked around with his flashlight. On the floor he saw a white cockatoo next to a broken bottle. The large white bird looked scared. It was the same white bird from before! But it got a weird look in its eyes as Sylvio got closer.

"Come here, poor little birdie," Sylvio said, "it's okay. I got you. I got you." He bent down to pick up the bird . . . but the bird had tricked him! It was a mean cockatoo named Nigel, and as soon as Sylvio was close enough, Nigel flew at his face and put a rag doused with sleeping gas into his mouth.

Sylvio choked and fainted.

Nigel stole Sylvio's keys. Then he went to the door of the Conservation Center and unlocked it, letting in a young, skinny boy. The boy was a bird smuggler. He was there to steal some of the birds!

Meanwhile, Blu didn't hear any of the noise—he was curled up trying to sleep.

But just then a scratching sound got his attention. The scratching was coming from Jewel, who was trying to pry open a vent.

"Arrrgh, excuse me, but I'm trying to sleep," Blu complained.

"Oh, *sorry*," said Jewel, "but *I'm* trying to escape."

"Escape?" asked Blu. "But why? This cage is awesome!"

"This cage . . ." said Jewel, looking surprised for a second. "Hah, oh," she squawked quietly. "What was I thinking? I wouldn't expect a *pet* to understand."

"What?" Blu said, sitting up and getting a little angry. "Pet? Did you just call me a pet? For the record, I am not a pet. I am a *companion*. And you know what? Do whatever you want because tomorrow morning Linda will come back for me and this whole nightmare will be over."

"Unbelievable." Jewel shook her head at Blu. "You'd rather be with a human than with your own kind."

"Well, that human has given me love and affection for the past fifteen years. My own

kind tried to strangle me after fifteen seconds."
Blu glared at Jewel.

She ruffled her feathers. "Yeah well, because of *them*, I've lost everything. You can't trust humans."

Just then Jewel heard a creaking sound and turned around. She saw the aviary door swinging open and darted toward it, excited to escape and fly free!

"Of course you can trust humans!" Blu called out as Jewel took off. "And I trust Linda. That's all that matters to me. Wait . . . Jewel? Jewel?"

Blu heard a muffled scream.

"Jewel?" A shadow passed over Blu and he shook with fear. "Oh, uh, hi there!" he stuttered, looking up into the shadow. "I, uh, *aaahhhh*!"

The shadowy man threw a sack over Blu and everything went black.

Meanwhile, Linda and Tulio were out at a beachside restaurant. They had no idea what was going on at the aviary. They were too busy having a good time enjoying the beautiful scenery and the faint sounds of music in the distance.

Tulio looked at Linda, who was a bit more nervous and awkward than the women of Rio. Linda adjusted her glasses and smiled. Tulio said, "It was kind of you to join me for dinner. I often eat alone. I mean, because of my work, of course."

"Yeah, Blu and I really don't go out much either," Linda agreed. "Especially not to incredible places like this!"

"This?" Tulio said, looking around the restaurant. "Oh, I am sure it is just like your restaurants in Moose Lake."

Linda almost laughed but just then a waiter came out with a huge knife, and she screamed! The waiter flashed the knife again and she saw a large piece of beef was skewered on it. He cut off some slices of meat for Linda.

"*Picanha!*" the waiter said as he handed her the meat.

From another side, a second waiter came over with a strange-looking plate, and shouted, "*Linguica!*" Then he lit the strange stuff on fire and shouted, *"Flambada!"* The flames of food exploded, leaving soot on Linda's glasses.

Just then, Tulio's phone rang. When he answered, a strange look passed across his face. Uh-oh. Bad news . . . Blu and Jewel had been kidnapped!

Linda and Tulio raced back to the Conservation Center. This was, by far, the very worst thing that had ever happened to Linda. Blu was her world—her everything—and now he was gone, and what did she have left? Nothing!

Linda sat on the stairs outside of the Conservation Center, as policemen hovered nearby, taking notes and asking Sylvio the guard questions. But so far they hadn't gotten any useful information.

Linda cried into the palms of her hands. "Oh, Blu," she sobbed. "This is all my fault. . . ." And she cried some more.

Tulio stood over her, not knowing what to do. He, too, was very upset. He put his arm on Linda's shoulder and tried to make her feel better. "No, Linda, no," he said, "this is not your fault."

Linda looked up at Tulio with tears in her

eyes. "You're right," she said. "It's not my fault. . . ." Suddenly, Linda got angry. It certainly wasn't her fault—because it wasn't even her idea to come here, was it?

Linda stood up, and turning toward Tulio, she said, "This is *your* fault! With your little bird talk and all that 'save the species' stuff!" Linda started making fun of how Tulio would talk in bird language, making ridiculous squawking sounds. "Well, ya know what I have to say to that? SQUAWK SQUAWK SQUAWK-ITY SQUAWK!" Linda had to stop to catch her breath. And when she did, she realized she'd been getting a bit carried away with her emotions.

"I'm sorry," Linda said. She could see how bad Tulio felt about the whole situation. She knew in her heart that it really wasn't his fault either. It was the fault of the evil bird smugglers!

Tulio shuffled his feet. "I just don't understand! Sylvio is the best guard in the business," he said.

He looked over at Sylvio, the big loveable guard. Linda looked over at him too. He was still wearing his silly Carnavale costume, and he was talking to a police officer.

The officer was doing his best to take down Sylvio's comments. "So let me get this straight," he said to Sylvio. "You were attacked by a . . . little . . . white . . . bird?" The policeman stared at Sylvio, who was so big and strong. How could a guy like him get taken down by a bird? It was nonsense!

"Yes!" exclaimed Sylvio. He held up the rag that the bird had used to put poison in his mouth. "He held this rag to my mouth! Like this!" At that, Sylvio put the rag back over his mouth. But then he breathed in the sleeping gas and fainted again. His big body fell to the ground like a rock. The policeman picked up the rag, and sniffed it to see if it had poison on it. It did, apparently, because he barely had time to make a face before he fainted on the spot.

Linda and Tulio looked at each other and sighed.

"We're doomed," said Linda.

CHAPTER

5

Meanwhile...

Blu and Jewel had been captured. Someone had put a cover on their cage, so they had no idea where they were! Jewel was able to tear a hole in the covering, and she poked her beak out. Jewel looked around while Blu paced nervously inside the cage.

"There's no place like home, there's no place like home," said Blu. "Oh, I wish I was back in my own cage with my mirror, and my swing, and my little bell. Oh how I miss my little bell. . . . "

"Shhh!" said Jewel, flopping quickly onto

her back. "Lie down like me and play dead," she whispered.

"What? I don't need to *play* dead. I'm about to have a heart attack anyway!"

"Just do it!" said Jewel.

"Fine." Blu sighed, but instead of copying Jewel, he started staggering around. Then he pretended to choke and gag and hold his chest—really pretending to die.

Jewel did not think this was funny at all. She stuck out her claw and grabbed Blu, pulling him down to the floor of the cage. "Stop twitching!" she whispered. "Stay quiet!"

As the birds were playing dead inside their cage, things were happening outside it. Someone picked up the cage from the back of a truck and opened a door into a big, old warehouse. The person holding the cage was Fernando, the young boy who had snuck into the aviary in the first place.

Inside the warehouse sat a whole gang of bird smugglers. The gang was led by Marcel, a very scary-looking man. Marcel's two friends, Tipa and Armando, stood behind him. Tipa and Armando were not very smart.

Armando shouted at Fernando. "Come on in, kid. Let's see what ya got."

Fernando stepped into the warehouse, still holding the cage.

Marcel smiled a nasty smile. "Well, what do you know?" he said. "Good work, Fernando! You see, boys . . . what did I tell you about this kid?"

Tipa cleared his throat. "You told us that you were going to pay him half as much as you said. . . . "

"No, you idiot!" said Marcel. "I said that he reminds me of myself when I was that age. Smart. Resourceful." He handed a bunch of bills to Fernando. "Here ya go, kid."

Fernando's face lit up when he saw the money, and his tummy grumbled a little— this money would buy his dinner. But then he counted them. "Hey!" he said to Marcel. "This is only half of what you promised me!"

"Ah, shut up, kid," Marcel said, distracted. He was staring eagerly at the cage. Slowly, he lifted off the cover, only to see . . .

Two dead birds! Well, not really dead, but Blu and Jewel sure *looked* dead.

Marcel was not pleased. "What the . . . ! I thought I told you I needed these birds alive! Tell me, Fernando, does this look alive to you? Huh?" Marcel reached into the cage and pulled out Jewel's limp body. Just then, Jewel snapped awake and bit Marcel's hand with her beak.

"Owwww!" said Marcel, letting go of Jewel, who flew madly toward a nearby window near the ceiling of the warehouse.

"Get her!" Marcel shouted at Tipa and Armando.

Blu peeked open his eyes as Tipa and Armando lumbered around the warehouse, trying to catch Jewel.

"Jewel!" cried Blu.

"Come here!" shouted Marcel, lunging after her.

Just as Jewel was about to fly to freedom, Nigel came out of nowhere and flew straight into her! He locked Jewel in his talons and held her against a pillar near the roof so she couldn't escape.

One of the evil bird's white feathers floated to the floor as he spoke. "Hello, pretty bird," he said to Jewel. "What's the matter? Cockatoo got your throat?"

Jewel tried to fight the white bird off, but she wasn't strong enough.

Marcel shouted to the white bird, "Nigel, you've got her! But keep her *alive*."

"Hmph," Nigel responded, swooping down with Jewel still in his claws, and then pushing her back into the cage.

Blu was shocked. "*That* was your plan? To just take off and leave me? Wow, thanks so much."

"Well," Jewel replied, clearly frustrated, "why didn't you follow me?"

Before Blu could think of a clever explanation to hide the real truth (that he was scared and didn't know how to fly), Marcel started talking to Nigel.

"Nice work, Nigel," he said, petting the white bird.

"Yeah," said Tipa. "Nice work, Nigel."

Marcel smiled to himself. "The last two blue Spix's Macaws on earth. These are worth a fortune!" Then Marcel put a chain on Blu's and Jewel's ankles. "These birds are so much more valuable as a set!" he said. Then he turned to Fernando. "Hey, Fernando, hang these up in the other room." He handed the cage with the chained-up Blu and Jewel inside to Fernando, who scuttled through a door into the other part of the warehouse.

When Fernando brought the cage through the door, Blu and Jewel noticed there were a lot more stolen birds there. In fact, there were lots and lots of cages, all full of different wild birds that had been captured. All of the birds looked miserable, hungry, and depressed.

"Let me out. Let me out. Let me out. Let me out," repeated one bird, over and over again.

"Pretty bird. Pretty bird. I'm a pretty bird. I'm a pretty bird." That was another one, who seemed more crazy than sad.

There was even a bat in the room! The bat kept saying, "I was framed! They got the wrong guy!"

Fernando walked farther into the room and found a spot for Blu and Jewel's cage. "Sorry, guys," he said to Blu and Jewel. "Nothing personal."

For a minute, Fernando stared at the cage, feeling a little bit bad for Blu and Jewel and all the other trapped birds. But he had a job to do. He worked for Marcel, after all, and this is what Marcel paid him to do—capture birds. So he put down the cage and walked out of the room.

Fernando went back to Marcel and asked, "So . . . what's gonna happen to them? Those new birds?"

Marcel grinned wickedly. "Oh, don't you worry," he said. "We're going to find good homes for them." Marcel started pushing Fernando toward the exit. "Now go on home to your mama."

"But I don't have a mama," said Fernando.

"A father?" asked Marcel.

Fernando shook his head no. But he was trying to think more about the delicious food he would be able to buy now that he had money. He was so hungry!

"Brother?" asked Armando.

Fernando shook his head again.

"Houseplant?" asked Tipa.

Fernando once again shook his head, feeling a little sad about the fact that he really had no one—he was all alone in the world.

"Aw," said Tipa, feeling sorry for Fernando. "Can we keep him, boss?"

Marcel just looked at the foolish, weepy-eyed Tipa, and shouted "No!"

Then he shoved poor Fernando out the door. Fernando took the money he made and left to get dinner. He went up to a rooftop to eat, but as he tried to get comfortable, he felt a tickle. He found a blue feather stuck in his shirt. Looking at the feather and thinking about what he'd done, Fernando suddenly wasn't hungry at all anymore.

CHAPTER

Back at the warehouse, Marcel was on the phone. "Of course I have *both* macaws. Yes, you were very clear. Tomorrow or the deal's off."

Armando was now watching television in the other room.

"Come on!" Armando called to Tipa. "The game is starting! Come on!"

Tipa came in and plopped down on the couch just as Marcel got ready to leave for the day. Marcel turned to them both and said, "All right, you two. Load the truck tonight. First

43

thing in the morning, we bring the birds to the airport. Got it?"

Armando and Tipa, who were both staring at the TV watching a soccer game, nodded and muttered, "Uh, yeah sure, sure, yeah. Uh-huh."

"Oh, and one of you feed Nigel," Marcel said. Upon hearing his name, Nigel fluttered his feathers and snapped at Tipa and Armando. They looked at each other nervously—they did not like Nigel. He was even meaner than Marcel. They both had lots of bandages on their fingers because of all the times Nigel had bitten them.

As soon as Marcel left the office, Tipa and Armando turned to each other and played Rock, Paper, Scissors, to see who would have to feed Nigel.

At the same time, they both shook their fists and said "Rock, paper, scissors, *shoot*!"

Tipa did "rock" while Armando did "scissors." Tipa won.

"Yes!" said Armando suddenly.

"Wait," Tipa whined. "I thought *I* won!"

But Armando pretended that scissors is

what beats rock.

"Well, I shoulda picked scissors!" Tipa said, as he began to unwrap a chicken leg. Then he held it out toward Nigel. That was Nigel's dinner. "Nice birdie!" said Tipa. "Here ya go."

All of a sudden, Nigel swooped down at Tipa, trying to get the chicken. Tipa screamed in fear and tried to cover his face with his hands as Nigel flew toward him and grabbed the chicken leg in his talons. Then Nigel flew up to the rafters to enjoy his feast. Tipa and Armando stared up at Nigel as he tore into the chicken meat.

"Ew," Tipa said, shaking his head. "Nigel's a total cannibal."

But then they heard cheering from the TV and realized they were missing a really good part of the soccer game. Right away, Tipa and Armando went back to the couch to get comfortable and watch TV.

Meanwhile, in the other part of the warehouse, Blu and Jewel were looking around at all the sad, exotic birds trapped inside. This was not good.

"Okay," said Blu, "pull it together. The key is not to panic."

"I'm not panicking," said Jewel.

"I wasn't talking to you," said Blu. "I was talking to *me*. It's gonna be okay. Linda will find us."

Jewel huffed, clearly annoyed with Blu. "Oh, great, and then she'll stick us behind another set of bars, right? Look, 'pet,' cages might work for you but I don't want to belong to anyone."

Just then Nigel flew into the room, his white feathers fluttering smoothly, carrying a chicken bone. He dragged the bone across all of the other birds' cages, making a rattling sound against the bars.

"Something seems to be lodged in my beak," said Nigel with a scary grin. He stopped in front of a cage full of tiny birds. They were babies and they were very afraid. "Would you mind helping me out?" Nigel said to the tiny birds, opening his beak wide at them.

There was a tiny piece of food at the back of Nigel's beak and one of the baby birds was brave enough to try to help him, while the others huddled in fear. As the braver baby bird leaned in to reach for the food—SNAP! Nigel closed his beak and the bird fell over backwards.

Nigel laughed at the baby birds. He liked making them afraid of him.

Then Nigel noticed Blu and Jewel. He remembered that they were the newest birds in the warehouse. Blu was watching all of this, and when Nigel turned his head toward Blu, Blu jumped back in shock.

"Oh I know I'm not a pretty birdie like *you*," said Nigel. "But I used to be quite a looker."

Nigel stepped to the side and pointed at a movie poster. On the poster was a bird that looked just like Nigel. It *was* Nigel, back when he was a younger, more handsome bird. Nigel used to be in movies!

"See?" said Nigel. "That's the funny thing about beauty. It's nearly impossible to make something ugly beautiful. But you can take a beautiful thing and make it ugly *just like that*." With a lightning-fast move, Nigel jumped in Jewel's face, showing one of his razor-sharp claws.

"Hey!" said Blu. "Leave her alone!"

"Sweet nightmares," said Nigel, and then he fluttered off.

"Not cool, man. Scary, but not cool," Blu said before turning to Jewel, "Are you okay?"

Jewel nodded. Then she took hold of two bars of their cage, and started to sway back and forth. The cage slowly started to rock with her.

Blu instantly got nervous. "Whoa!!! Whoa, whoa, wait, wait, wait. What are you doing?" he squeaked.

"Getting us out of here," said Jewel.

"No, no, no. Wait! All the survival guides say to sit and wait and help will come."

Jewel just stared at Blu. He was clearly in denial. "No one is coming! We're on our own!" she hissed.

CHAPTER

Back inside the office, Tipa and Armando were still watching the soccer game on TV, and Nigel was perched in the rafters, watching them.

"Yes, yes, yes!" Tipa and Armando both cried, getting excited about the game. It was at a really good part. Tipa and Armando were so into the match that they didn't even hear the crashing sounds coming from the next room— but Nigel did.

Nigel swooped down and turned off the TV. *Someone* had to alert these idiots to the fact that the birds in the warehouse were trying to escape!

"Nooooooo!" shouted Tipa and Armando. "Nigel, what are you doing? Get back here, bird!"

Nigel stole the remote control and flew away.

Just then, in the other part of the warehouse, Jewel rocked their cage so hard that it hit the wall with a loud BANG!

"Stop!" Blu said. "Why are you rocking the cage when you could just open the door?" And with that, Blu reached his wing around and flicked open the latch, sliding the cage door open.

Jewel stared at Blu in amazement.

"How did you . . . "

"It's easy. Just a standard Phillips slide bolt. Just rotate the latch and pull back on the—"

"Come on!" Jewel shouted at Blu. "There's no time. Let's fly!"

Jewel tried to fly, but Blu was still dragging on the chain attached to her ankle. He clung to the bars with his beak.

"What are you doing?" cried Jewel.

"Well, I can't fl . . ." mumbled Blu, with the bar of the cage still in his beak.

Jewel pulled on the chain again and tried to fly. "Can't what?!" she screamed at Blu.

Just as Tipa, Armando, and Nigel came into the room, Blu finally let go of the cage with his beak as Jewel yanked on the chain. As they started to fall, Blu finished his sentence: "Can't *flyyyyyy*!"

The cage shot out of Blu's grip and hit Nigel in the head.

Both Blu and Jewel soared through the window together, into the outside world, and then they both screamed as they went plummeting down, down, down.

As they fell, screaming, Blu and Jewel caught onto a clothesline, and zipped along it until they hit the wall and crashed down to another clothesline.

Jewel scowled at Blu. "I hate you."

They fell off that clothesline and then through a series of clotheslines before hitting the ground outside the warehouse with a hard thump.

"You couldn't have told me this before now?" Jewel snapped at Blu.

"Okay, fine!" said Blu. "Yes, I can't fly. I pick my beak, and once in a while, I pee in the bird-bath. Are you happy?"

Blu suddenly realized they were not alone—there were crowds of people bustling about, all around them in the street.

"Ahhh!" said Blu, feeling overwhelmed by all of the commotion.

"Hey, snap out of it," said Jewel. "Look, they're after us!" Jewel pointed with her wing, and Blu saw that Tipa and Armando had come out of the warehouse. They were looking for him and Jewel.

"We gotta get out of here," Jewel commanded, quickly pulling Blu along with her. But it was really hard to walk when their ankles were tied together with a chain.

Blu joined in. "Stop. Just stop. Listen to me: Inside leg, outside leg. Inside-outside-inside-outside," he instructed.

Together they chanted, "Inside-outside-inside-outside," over and over as they tried to weave through the crowds, waddling as quickly as they could.

They dashed through a café where lots of people were watching the same soccer game that Tipa and Armando had been watching on TV. Everyone in the café was shouting and cheering at the television as the birds dashed in.

Close on their tail feathers were Tipa and Armando—and they were getting closer by the second. Then Blu saw a cat lying on the counter, and he got an idea. As he ran by, he made a loud barking sound at the cat. The cat didn't see the birds, but it did hear the bark, and got scared.

"Yow!" went the cat, and leaped up—straight into Tipa's face.

That slowed Tipa and Armando down a bit.

"It pays to be bilingual," said Blu, smiling as he and Jewel continued to run. "I bet you didn't know I could speak dog."

Meanwhile, Nigel was soaring above the busy crowds, trying to spot Blu and Jewel.

"This is just great. I'm chained to the only bird in the world who can't fly!" Jewel shouted in frustration.

"Actually," Blu began as he and Jewel dashed in the direction of a fruit seller, "I have done quite a bit of research and there are about forty species of flightless birds."

"And you're not one of them!" said Jewel.

Blu looked up and saw Nigel. Looking up got him out of rhythm with Jewel, and both of them tumbled down a bunch of stairs, landing in a pile of old, dirty tires. They bounced off the tires and were spun around in circles. Then they hit a drainpipe and slid down it until a piece of the pipe snapped and the birds were flung through another open window.

Blu and Jewel landed in a family's apartment. The family members were all gathered around watching the same soccer game on TV and shouting at the screen as Blu and Jewel bounced through the window. Tipa and Armando were still following—and they still were not far behind. No one noticed the commotion because the whole family was so intent on watching the game!

Once back outside of the apartment, Blu and Jewel made their way to the rooftops. There, they slid from one apartment roof to another. Tipa and Armando were hot on their trail, and Nigel was still flying over them.

As they passed by many houses and restaurants and buildings, they could see that everyone inside was watching the soccer game on TV. It really was an exciting game! In fact, anywhere you might go in Rio on that day, you would have seen more and more people watching this game. In Brazil, this was *the* game. The game everybody had to watch. Even Tipa and Armando gave up their chase in order to get back to the television. Everyone in Rio was waiting to see who was going to win, and the excitement was growing as the game neared its end.

Meanwhile, Nigel flew closer and closer to Blu and Jewel. But just as Nigel darted toward them, Blu veered to the side. As a result, Nigel flew straight into an electric transformer. There was a spark of electricity, and Nigel squawked as a cloud of gray feathers *poof*ed out the other end. Nigel had broken the transformer, and all of the power in the city shut off. Which meant that all of the televisions in the entire area stopped working—all at once. Which meant that everyone watching the game was now standing in the dark in their apartments or in a café, unable to see the end of the game.

"NOOOOOOOOOOOOO!!!!!!!" The cry echoed through Rio as everybody screamed at their broken televisions.

Blu and Jewel escaped into the forest at the edge of town.

CHAPTER

8

Jewel and Blu were relieved that they had escaped the horrible bird smugglers' warehouse and had found the dense jungle outside of town.

They still had to walk with the chain stuck to both of their ankles. Jewel was exhausted. Blu, however, was terrified. The jungle was a scary place, especially as it started to get dark.

"Oh! What was that?" Blu shouted when he heard a sudden noise.

Jewel ignored him and kept walking. It was just the sound of a stick breaking.

"Wait, what about that noise?" Blu said.

"Just a rock this time," said Jewel.

"Wait, oh gosh," said Blu, freezing in place. "I feel something on my back. Is it a giant spider?"

"No, silly," said Jewel. "It's just a big, green leaf." But really, it was a spider. And the spider was just about to bite Blu when Jewel brushed it off and it fell away. "Just a leaf," Jewel said again. "Told ya. Now let's find a safe place to sleep."

"Safe?" said Blu. "We're in the jungle. You know when people say 'It's a jungle out there'? Well I'm pretty sure they don't mean it as a good thing."

"Listen, I hate to break it to you," Jewel said, looking Blu in the eye, "but this is where our kind naturally lives."

"Hey, don't talk to me about nature," said Blu. "I watch *Animal Planet*. I know all about the food chain." They walked by as a fly was eaten by a frog which was then devoured by a snake.

"You see?" said Blu as they hurried on. "Out here, I'm just a snack. Nothing more than a feathery spring roll."

"That is why normally we stay in the trees and not on the ground," Jewel said.

Blu looked up at a tree—a really big one. In fact, it looked strangely familiar. Kind of like a tree he remembered from long ago . . . kind of like the tree he first fell from, when he was just a baby chick, fifteen years ago. Could it be?

No way. It couldn't be.

Blu shook his head. "I'd be much more comfortable in something man-made." Just then Blu noticed something. It was a wooden gazebo built in a clearing of the trees, just at the edge of a cliff.

"Ugh," said Jewel. "I can't believe I am going to have to drag your butt all the way up there."

"Drag me? Just wait. Watch and learn," said Blu.

Blu started to climb quickly up the side of the gazebo, climbing around the tower with power and ease.

"Wait, what are you . . . *ahhh*!" cried Jewel as Blu grabbed onto one piece of wood and swung Jewel around to another one.

dragging whose butt now, huh?"

_____ roudly.

"_____ a, very funny," Jewel grumbled.

_____ the time they reached the top of the wooden gazebo, Jewel was exhausted and her feathers were very ruffled—which she did not care for much at all.

"See?" said Blu, standing at the very top. "Who needs flying?"

"Birds. Birds need flying," Jewel answered. "Flying is . . . it's freedom. It means you never have to rely on anyone else. Don't you want that?"

"I don't know," said Blu. "Sounds a little lonely, actually."

Blu and Jewel sat back on the top of the wooden gazebo. They could see all the way over the jungle, to the town beyond. The city was dark because of the power blackout that had been caused by Nigel crashing into the transformer.

In fact, the only light at all was the light from the full, round moon.

Jewel gazed into the darkness.

All of a sudden, the power came back on

and the whole city lit up with windows and streetlamps and flashing signs. It was beautiful.

Jewel yawned. "Let's get some sleep," she said, trying to relax.

"I'm probably gonna be up for a little while. I'm still on Minnesota time," said Blu, as Jewel closed her eyes and got settled.

"Well, good night," said Jewel.

"Good night, Jewel," said Blu. Then he looked out over the city again, and said, although she couldn't hear him, "Good night, Linda."

CHAPTER

9

Early the next morning, the sounds of the city were still hushed as Fernando, the boy who had helped Marcel steal the exotic birds, walked through the streets. Fernando passed a paper sign taped to a wall. It showed a picture of Linda and Blu from Halloween a few years back. The sign read, HAVE YOU SEEN MY BIRD?

Fernando ripped the sign off of the building and stood there staring at it. He felt terrible about what he'd done. He needed the money, but he was really sick of working for Marcel. It was time to put a stop to it.

* * *

Meanwhile, at Marcel's warehouse, Marcel was furious with Tipa and Armando. He couldn't believe his two stupid but strong thugs had allowed Blu and Jewel to escape. Those were extremely valuable birds! He could sell them for lots of money!

"They were two birds, chained together, in a *cage*!" Marcel shouted at Tipa and Armando. "How could you just lose them?"

"They outsmarted us, boss!" answered Tipa dutifully.

Armando just nodded.

Marcel walked back and forth, thinking, getting more and more angry.

"But don't worry," Tipa said to Marcel. "We'll get them back. I have a plan!"

"Oh, great," said Marcel. "What are you going to do, wander the whole city calling, 'Here, birdie birdie! Here, birdie!?'"

"Um . . . ," muttered Tipa. Actually, that *was* his plan, but he didn't want to tell Marcel that now. "Well, anything sounds dumb when you say it like *that*."

Marcel picked up Blu and Jewel's empty cage and smashed it onto Tipa's head. Tipa winced from the pain and stopped talking.

"Okay," Marcel said, now trying to calm himself down. "We have to get the birds to the airport tonight."

"But it's Carnavale!" Tipa cried, still rubbing his head. "All the roads will be blocked by the parade."

"That's why I wanted to leave this morning!" Marcel shook his fist at Tipa, then stopped. "Nigel!" he called.

Nigel came swooping into the room. He was a little bit dirty and scarred from his encounter with the transformer, but otherwise he looked as evil as ever.

Marcel pointed at Nigel and smiled his scary, nasty smile. "This bird is ten times smarter than the two of you combined," he said, looking at Armando and Tipa.

"Well," said Tipa, "if he's so smart then why don't you put him in charge?"

"I *am* putting him in charge," said Marcel.

Armando turned his head to Tipa and opened his eyes wide. "Stop suggesting things!" he whispered loudly to Tipa.

Marcel pet Nigel's head. "Go, find the

runaway birds." He opened the warehouse door and Nigel flew into the air. Marcel watched as Nigel soared off to find Blu and Jewel.

Then Marcel turned back to Tipa and Armando. They could already hear the sounds of people starting to party and dance in the streets for Carnavale. There would be a big parade soon enough.

"If we can't get *through* the parade," Marcel said to the two other men, "then we'll just have to be *in* the parade."

Back at the Conservation Center, Fernando had come all the way from the heart of the city, carrying the poster of Linda and Blu in his hand. When he finally got there he saw Linda and Tulio sleeping on the steps outside, with a pile of posters scattered all around them. They'd been up most of the night hanging signs and posters, hoping to find Blu and Jewel.

As Fernando walked up, Linda was still dreaming, muttering, "Have you seen my bird? Squawking . . . blue feathers . . ."

"Lady!" said Fernando, waking up Linda and Tulio. "American lady!"

"Blu?" said Linda, rubbing her eyes. She realized she had a flyer stuck to her face, and pulled it off her cheek. She also had a sunburn from sleeping outside in the hot morning sun.

"Where?" said Tulio, perking up.

"I know where your birds are!" said Fernando eagerly.

Suddenly Linda was wide awake. "You found Blu?" she asked excitedly. "Are you sure?"

Fernando held up a blue feather.

Linda gasped. "It's his!" The feather definitely belonged to her bird, and for the first time in twenty-four hours, Linda started to feel hope again.

Tulio stood up. "Let me see that." He took the feather and licked it. Then he stuck the whole feather in his mouth! "Hmmm," he said, thinking as he tasted the feather. Then he gasped too. "You're right!" he exclaimed. "It *is* Blu's!"

"Okay, so where is he?" Linda asked Fernando.

"Come on, let's go. I'll take you to him," Fernando answered. He started to walk off and Linda quickly followed him, but then Tulio stopped her.

"No, no, no, Linda. Linda, wait. We don't know this boy. We can't trust him," Tulio warned.

Linda gave Tulio a stern look. "I *have* to trust him. I don't have a choice." She knew, in her heart, that she would do anything—follow anyone—if it meant saving Blu.

CHAPTER

First thing in the morning, Blu and Jewel set about trying to break the chain that bound them together. The hot Rio sun was already pouring through the forest trees, and from one of those trees Blu had attached a long vine. At the other end of the vine he had tied a large rock.

Now Blu and Jewel were pulling on the vine, trying to lift the rock.

"Are you sure about this plan?" Jewel asked Blu, raising one of her bird eyebrows.

"Yes, I've figured out all the math," Blu

answered, showing Jewel where he had drawn some equations in the dirt.

"Okaaaayyyy," Jewel said and sighed, helping Blu lift the big rock higher.

"After this, we can go find Linda," Blu said.

"No, *you* can go find Linda," Jewel said. "Once this chain is off I'm going to go back to being free in the jungle. Deal?"

"Fine. Deal," Blu said, but when he reached out to shake wings with Jewel, the loop slipped out of his grasp, snagged on his beak, and dragged him into the branches. Jewel, chained to him, was yanked up after him. They hit the tree branches and fell to the ground with a thud.

"Nice try, genius," said Jewel.

Blu didn't answer. He heard rustling in the bushes nearby. Through the branches of the bush, Blu could see two pairs of eyes staring at him.

Uh-oh.

Blu whispered, "Something's watching us!" He started to get really scared. . . .

But then, out of the bushes emerged two cute baby toucans! Their names were Miguel and Rita, and they toddled over to Blu and Jewel, smiling. They jumped up and down.

"Oh careful, Blu," Jewel said sarcastically. "I mean, who knows, they might try to cuddle you to death!"

Blu ignored Jewel's comment. The two toucan chicks were so cute! "Awww," Blu said, leaning down to them. "Come here, little ones."

But as he got closer, one of the chicks put its beak into Blu's chest . . . and started ripping off his feathers!

"Aaaahhhhhhh!" Blu shouted. "You little—"

"Intruders!" shouted the toucan chick. "Attack!"

The second baby toucan climbed up Jewel's back and covered her eyes while pulling her feathers.

"Ow, quit it!" Jewel cried. Jewel and Blu ran around trying to escape the angry little chicks.

Pretty soon, Jewel and Blu had gotten all tangled up in their chain.

One of the baby toucans pointed at Jewel and Blu, now that they were trapped. "Kill them!" shouted the chick. Then a bunch of other chicks came out of the bushes and all started jumping onto Jewel and Blu.

"Help!" Blu called out.

Just then, an older toucan called down from the trees. "What's going on down there?" The older bird was named Rafael. He was colorful, with a very kind face. He started to fly down when he saw that Blu and Jewel were covered in a bunch of angry toucan chicks.

"Shoo!" said Rafael to the chicks.

All the chicks looked up and said, "Daddy! Daddy! We got 'em!"

"Okay, guys, okay!" Rafael said, laughing. All the chicks jumped off of Jewel and Blu and ran over to Rafael. They started climbing all over him and tickling him. Rafael laughed some more.

Rafael was laughing so hard he could barely talk. "I have told you a thousand times . . . ," he said to his chicks. "Manoela! Sophia! Come on now! Stop!" He laughed as the chicks continued to tickle their dad.

In the meantime, Jewel and Blu had managed to untangle themselves.

Jewel smirked at Rafael. "Seems like you're in a little over your head," she said.

"Kids!" Rafael said, shrugging. "They're giving me gray feathers." Rafael looked up into the branches and saw two more of his chicks, Marco and Carlos, playing with an egg. "Hey!" Rafael shouted at them. "He's not a maraca! Stop shaking him!"

Then Rafael looked back at Jewel and Blu and sighed. "I need a break! So, you two love-birds headed to Carnavale?" he asked them.

"Whoa," said Jewel. "Lovebirds? I don't *think* so!"

"Um," said Blu. "We only just met a couple days ago. We're more like acquaintance birds."

"And not even that," Jewel said. "More like chained to each other birds. Speaking of which, do you think you could help us get this thing off?" she asked, holding up the chain.

Rafael thought for a second and then his face lit up as an idea hit him. "Lucky for you!" he said. "You know Rafael, and Rafael knows everyone!"

But before Rafael could say anything more, one of the chicks poked him in the eye.

"Ow!" Rafael yelled. "Again with the eye! Okay kids, do you want me to call your mother over?"

As soon as Rafael mentioned their mom, all the chicks stopped playing around and poking him. They all ran away and hid in the bushes again.

"Hah," said Rafael to Jewel and Blu. "Works every time. They're scared to death of their mom." Rafael winked.

Just as Rafael said this, the mom, named Eva, came flying down. She stood right behind Rafael. "Call me for what?" Eva asked.

"Eva, my love," Rafael said. "I must take this young couple to see Luiz!"

Eva squinted and looked Rafael in the eyes. She was not a toucan to be easily tricked. "You don't fool me for a second. You're not going to find Luiz, are you? You're just going to find your friends so you can sneak off to Carnavale and party!"

"Oh, Carnavale! That magical place where I once met the most beautiful bird in the world . . . ," Rafael said, batting his eyelashes at his wife.

But Eva turned away in a huff. Sure, she had met her husband at Carnavale. But Carnavale was a wild party, and now she didn't like the idea of Rafael going off there to have fun, while she was stuck at home!

Eva raised her eyebrow at Rafael. "That was eighteen eggs ago," she said.

"Ah, but I still remember the song that was playing when I first laid eyes on you," Rafael said to her. He wrapped his wings around Eva and started humming. Eva started to grin, despite herself.

Rafael started singing, "Tall and tan and young and lovely, the girl from Ipanema goes walking . . . Come on, baby! Sing it with me."

But when Eva started singing, it sounded more like squawking. She was a terrible singer! The funny thing was that Rafael didn't seem to notice. He loved his wife so much he didn't even care that she had a horrible voice.

"Ah," said Rafael. "Your singing is like a river of the sweetest honey."

Finally, Eva gave in. "Fine," she said to Rafael. "Take these birds to Luiz. Just hurry back, okay?"

"You're an angel," said Rafael. "I'll miss you, my little mango muffin."

"I'll miss you, too, my coconut cupcake," Eva said.

Then some of the chicks started to make trouble in the nest and Eva flew off to scold them. "Marco! Carlos! Leave your brother alone!" And then she was gone.

After Eva flew off, Rafael and Jewel and Blu headed off on their journey to find the mysterious Luiz.

"I can't believe she actually let me go!" Rafael said happily as they walked.

"So," said Blu. "Who is this Luiz and how far away is he?"

"Oh not far," said Rafael. "Maybe thirty minutes as the crow flies." He pointed into the distance.

"And how long as the macaw walks?" Blu asked.

Jewel smirked at Rafael. "Bobo here can't fly," she said, pointing at Blu.

"But, he's a *bird*!" Rafael exclaimed.

Blu bristled. "Not all birds fly, ya know. There's ostriches . . ."

"You're not an ostrich," Jewel said.

"Well, not technically!" Blu was getting embarrassed as usual.

Rafael interrupted. "Wait-wait-wait-wait-wait. My friends, I want to help, but walk the whole way? It can't be done!"

But then Rafael looked back at Eva, who was flying around trying to gather all of their misbehaving chicks. Then he shrugged. He'd rather help Jewel and Blu than have to deal with his chicks right now.

"Ah well," Rafael said, smiling. "I guess we could give it a shot!"

And off they went, heading deep into the forest.

CHAPTER

Back in Rio, the city streets were starting to get very busy, and Nigel was flying about in search of Jewel and Blu. He was determined to bring them back to Marcel.

As Nigel soared through the city, he spotted a group of tourists being entertained by dancing marmosets, a type of monkey. The marmosets danced around in the street and the tourists laughed and snapped pictures. But then all of a sudden, one of the marmosets stole a tourist man's watch.

The tourists weren't laughing anymore.

"Hey, that's my watch!" the man called as the marmosets scampered along the streets, snickering.

Nigel was watching all of this, and soon he swooped down in front of the marmoset that had the watch. He was a large marmoset, but Nigel was not afraid of him.

"Hello, boys," Nigel said to the marmosets. "Seems like you've had a busy day." He looked around and saw that the marmosets had stolen more than just a watch. There were all sorts of jewelry pieces, coins, and other shiny objects the marmosets had stolen from people on the streets.

"What, this stuff?" said the large marmoset, the one with the watch still in his hand. "Oh, this is just stuff we found. Right, boys?" He was clearly the leader of the other monkeys.

"Yeah," said the other marmosets. "Yeah sure, sure, like you said."

Nigel fluttered his dirty white feathers. "I'm not interested in your nicked knickknacks. Your burgled baubles bore me. No. I'll tell you what I need. There are two blue macaws out there, and I need you to help me find them. You have friends all over the city, and those friends have eyes. I want everyone on the lookout for these birds. They're very valuable."

"Oh yeah?" asked the big marmoset. "What's in it for us?"

"That's a fair question," said Nigel. Then Nigel swooped closer and grabbed the leader marmoset by his tail, lifting him high, high in the air. All of the marmoset's jewelry made loud jangling noises as it fell off of him. It turned out the biggest marmoset wasn't really so big—he just had lots of things hidden in his clothes. After Nigel shook him upside down, it was clear the marmoset looked just like all the other marmosets. He was skinny and scared.

"Let's discuss what's in it for you," Nigel said with a snarl. He dangled the leader, about to drop him. Then he let go.

The marmoset screamed as Nigel let him fall toward to the ground.

Nigel flew downward next to the marmoset. "I certainly see your point," Nigel said, smiling his evil smile. "But I just don't see what I can possibly do for you."

"Okay, okay, we'll do it! Just save me!

Please, save me!" the marmoset shrieked, still falling.

"Good," Nigel said, catching him by the tail again just before the marmoset crashed into the ground.

The marmoset sighed. "Thank you!"

"Now then," said Nigel, looking around at all the other marmosets. "Any more questions?"

All the marmosets shook their heads, terrified of Nigel.

"Good," said Nigel again. "Spread out and find these macaws by the end of the day—or else it's flying lessons for everyone. Now go!"

The marmosets scampered off in all directions as Nigel smiled to himself and flew back toward the warehouse.

The marmosets would bring Blu and Jewel back to him. And then he'd deliver the annoying blue birds to Marcel, and Marcel would sell them, and they'd all be rich in the end.

Nigel laughed to himself as he flew through the air. *I hope those two birds are scared*, he thought. *Because they should be.*

CHAPTER

12

Rafael led Blu and Jewel over to a high ledge at the edge of the cliffs, where hang gliders liked to jump and then glide through the air and over the jungle, over the beautiful canopy of trees. The view was breathtaking, but Blu was nervous. Jewel and Rafael were planning to teach him how to fly. It was the only way they'd make it to Luiz, who could help them remove the chain that tied Blu and Jewel together.

"I've changed my mind," said Blu. "I'm not ready. Maybe we can just find a bus schedule or something."

"Come on," Rafael whispered. "You're not gonna back out now—in front of the lady?"

Blu looked at Jewel. He really didn't want to seem like a coward.

"Uh, okay. Yeah. Yeah, sure, this is good."

"All right, that's the spirit!" said Rafael, thumping Blu on the back.

Jewel glanced at Blu, who was shaking with fear. "You sure you're up to this?"

Blu stood up taller. "Yeah! Yeah, I mean . . . it's not like we're just hurling ourselves off a mountain or something." He chuckled nervously. "Right?"

"Actually," Rafael said, nodding, "that was pretty much my entire plan."

Blu was shocked. "What?!"

"Oh don't worry, Blu," said Rafael. "Flying is in your DNA! And if our featherless friends can do it, how hard can it be?" he asked, pointing at a person hang gliding across the canopy.

"Okay," Rafael continued. "I need you two to get closer. Closer. Closer. Ooh, nice!" he said after nudging Blu and Jewel next to each other. "Now, put your feathers around each other."

"What?" said Blu.

"Come on, amigo!" said Rafael. "It's not like she's gonna bite!"

Then Rafael paused and looked at Jewel. "Will you?" he asked her.

"We'll see," said Jewel.

"Now," Rafael commanded, "you flap your right wing, and you flap your left wing, and together, you two fly!"

Blu stammered, "This doesn't seem aerodynamically possible. . . ."

Rafael threw up his wings. "*Ai, ai, ai, ai, ai!* You think too much. Flying is not what you think up here," he said, pointing to his head. "It's what you feel in here," he continued, patting his heart. "And when you feel the rhythm of your heart, you fly. . . ."

Rafael backed up to the edge of the cliff and spread his wings as he dove backward into the air and then disappeared.

Blu gasped. But then Rafael popped back up over the edge of the cliff, flapping his wings. "See!" he said. "It's easy!"

"Easy?" asked Blu. "Easy for *you* to say. 'Cause from here it looks *really* hard."

Jewel shook her head at Blu. "Hey, if you want to see Linda again, this is the only way," she said.

"Okay, you're right." Blu sighed.

"Yes, I am."

"This is for Linda," Blu said, nodding.

"Right." Jewel nodded.

"Keep it simple."

She shrugged. "Easy breezy."

Blu practiced his moves. "Thrust, lift, drag . . ."

"Oh, come on!" Jewel shouted, losing her patience. "Let's go!" She yanked Blu and they started running toward the edge of the cliff, each flapping the opposite wing while holding onto each other.

"Woah, woah, *wait*!!" Blu squawked. "I can't do it!"

Blu stopped short, but Jewel kept going, which meant that the chain pulled Blu's leg out from under him.

"Oh, no, not again!" Jewel said, looking behind her too late. They both squawked and screamed as they went falling off the edge of the cliff.

* * *

Blu and Jewel were falling, falling, falling . . . and then suddenly, they were gliding seamlessly through the air. WHOOSH!

"Am I dead?" Blu shouted over the sound of the air as they flew through it.

"No, we're still alive. Ha, ha!" Jewel answered, pointing down.

They had landed on top of a hang glider, and they were sailing through the sky on top of him.

Blu laughed with relief. Then he looked around him. And his beak dropped open and his eyes became wide.

Wow. Soaring through the clouds so high, Blu could see the whole city spreading out ahead.

"This is the most gorgeous thing I've ever seen," Blu said.

"See what you've been missing?" Jewel said.

"Yeah."

Rafael showed up, flying beside them. "All right, Blu!" he called over. "You're flying. Sort of. Not really, but do you feel it?"

"Yes, I do feel it!" Blu called back.

Jewel spread her wings and closed her eyes, enjoying the wind on her feathers. Blu was watching her, and soon, he did the same thing. It felt great. Pretty soon, his feet lifted slightly off of the glider's back.

Wait a second! Was Blu . . . could it be . . . was he actually flying?

Jewel's eyes popped open. "No, Blu. Wait!"

Surprised, Blu leaned back, but with the power of the wind, both he and Jewel went tumbling off the back of the glider.

"*Ay caramba!*" cried Rafael, flying after them.

Blu and Jewel hit one hang glider and then another as they tumbled through the sky. Finally, they hit one hang glider right in the face! The glider panicked, and they all went plummeting.

"We're gonna die!" Blu wailed as they clung to the glider's face and fell, faster and faster.

Down on the beach, lots of people were enjoying the beautiful day, when all of a sudden they saw a strange object falling from the sky.

It was a hang glider, with two birds clinging to his face.

Everybody screamed and dashed for cover. Blu, Jewel, and the hang glider spiraled down onto the beach, bouncing off of the top of a beach umbrella. Blu and Jewel spun into a volleyball net, then onto a surfboard, and finally they slid out onto the sand.

Rafael swooped down onto the sand beside Blu and Jewel, and furrowed his brows at Blu. "You did not feel it in here," he said, beating his heart.

Still spitting out sand, Jewel gave a sarcastic snort. "Ya think?"

"All right," Rafael went on. "Come on. *Vamanos*, you two. We've got a ride to catch!" Just then a coconut truck started to drive away. Blu and Jewel ran to catch up with Rafael. "Come on, lovebirds!" Rafael cried. Jewel jumped effortlessly on to the back of the truck, but Blu was left dragging behind. As the truck neared a corner, Jewel noticed Blu was missing. She leaned out and pulled him up to safety just as they turned the corner, passing the very jeep that Tulio was driving.

CHAPTER

13

The coconut truck carried Blu, Jewel, and Rafael into the heart of Rio. It dumped all the coconuts—along with Jewel and Blu—into a street just outside the marketplace.

Rafael swooped down beside them. "Now all we have to do is find Luiz!" he said. Just as he was saying that, two birds flew by who recognized him. They were Pedro and Nico. Rafael was an old friend of theirs, and when they noticed Blu with Rafael, they remembered that they had seen Blu in his cage when he first arrived in Rio.

"Hold up!" said Pedro. "Rewind! Ain't that the bird from the cage?"

Nico chirped. "Yeah, you were on lockdown!" Then he and Pedro noticed Jewel.

Pedro whistled, impressed. "You work fast, bird! You was locked up and now you rollin' with a hot wing. Whoo! I want to be like you!"

Blu felt himself blushing. "Oh, it's not what you think, we're just chained together."

"Hey, I'm not judging," said Nico, laughing.

"What he is *trying* to say is that we are not together!" Jewel said, ruffling her feathers, annoyed.

"Ah, really?" said Nico. "Then move aside, Clyde, cause baby got beak. . . ." he said, admiring how pretty Jewel was.

Jewel rolled her eyes. "Can we go find Luis now?"

"Luis? He just left," they told her. "He took the trolley back to the garage."

"Oh, great." Jewel sighed.

"Relax, baby bird," Nico cooed. "You can catch the next one."

"And you know what that means," said Pedro. "Time to shake your tail feathers at the club!"

And with that, Pedro and Nico led Rafael, Blu, and Jewel through a secret entrance into a bird club. Inside the club, loud music was playing and lots of birds were having a great time talking, dancing, and singing.

Little did they know that just outside the club, the marmosets had spotted them, and were about to go report back to Nigel.

"Some party, huh?" cried Rafael, excited to be back at the club where he used to spend so much time as a younger bird.

"It's the coolest place I've ever seen!" Blu admitted.

Just then, Nico and Pedro went onstage to sing a song. Everyone cheered and shouted.

At first, Blu just stood there taking it all in. But soon, the rhythm started to get to him. He began to tap his foot. Then he wiggled his butt. Pretty soon, he wanted to dance like he'd never danced before. Blu was drawn toward the music, and he dragged Jewel out on to the dance floor with him.

Jewel laughed. "What are you doing?"

"I don't know!" Blu answered.

Pretty soon, the crowd was cheering for Blu, who was dancing joyfully in the middle. Even Rafael was impressed with Blu's moves.

"All right, Blu! Nice!" he shouted, clapping along.

Jewel shrugged and finally started dancing along with Blu. Then she started singing along with the music. Everyone was stunned—Jewel had the most amazing voice!

"I think she likes you," Rafael said in a loud whisper.

"What? Are you kidding?" said Blu. "No way."

Between their awesome singing and dancing, Blu and Jewel were tearing it up and everyone was cheering and loving it. It was the best day of Blu's life.

Until . . .

The ceiling of the club broke open.

And the marmosets came crashing down.

CHAPTER

14

The marmosets tore through the club, and the music came screeching to a halt. They formed a circle around Blu and Jewel.

Then the big marmoset stepped forward—the leader. He pointed at the two blue macaws that stood frozen in place, the chain between them trembling.

"You two are coming with me!" he said.

"Over my dead body," Jewel said fiercely.

The big marmoset smiled. "That can be arranged."

Rafael tried to break through the ring of

marmosets and marched up to the leader. "Come on," he said in a friendly voice. "Let's just all relax here, okay? I'm sure we can talk this out. . . ."

The marmoset started to slap Rafael, but then Kipo, the large bird who owned the place, stepped up.

"Now I'm angry. This is *my* club," Kipo said. "You mess with my friends, you mess with me."

"And me!" said Rafael.

"And us!" said Nico and Pedro.

"And us!" cried all of the other birds in the club.

The leader of the marmosets pointed at all the birds and shouted, "Get them!"

All of the monkeys lunged into the crowd, fighting the birds.

The big marmoset grabbed Blu and tossed him aside. As Blu went through the air, the chain swung Jewel around, and she crashed straight into another marmoset, taking him down.

When Blu and Jewel realized that their chain could help them fight the marmosets, they leaped into action, swinging each other around the room, knocking into one marmoset after another.

"This way!" said Blu.

"Nice one!" said Jewel.

The whole club had erupted into a crazy fight between the birds and the marmosets, when all of a sudden, through the commotion, they heard a loud sound:

CLANG! CLANG!

It was the trolley bell.

"The trolley!" Blu cried.

"Come on!" said Jewel. "We gotta get outta here and find Luiz!"

They leaped out of the club and into the street. But then they looked over and saw the trolley starting to leave. They looked at each other, panicked.

Out of nowhere, Kipo flew over them. He swooped down and picked up both Blu and Jewel with his enormous beak. He carried them over all the chaos in the streets and dropped them safely onto the trolley.

"Good-bye!" Kipo called to them, as the trolley rolled away along the tracks. "And good luck!"

 94

CHAPTER

RIO RIO RIO RIO RIO RIO RIO RIO

15

Little did they know that at just that moment, Tulio's jeep was driving through town with Linda and Fernando inside. People were dressed in Carnavale costumes and dancing all through the streets, making it impossible for Tulio to get anywhere.

Stuck in too much traffic, they all hopped out of the jeep. Fernando spotted a motorcycle. He ran over, talked quickly with its owner, and then hopped on and started driving it. Linda jumped on behind him, and Tulio got on, clutching Linda for dear life. They weaved in and out of the dancers and the other cars in the streets, speeding along toward the center of the city, where the parade was beginning.

"Hey, kid," Tulio shouted through the wind to Fernando. "How did you get this bike anyway?"

"I traded it for your jeep!" Fernando said with a wink.

"What?!"

"It's in great shape!" Fernando said.

Tulio sat back, clinging to Linda and trying to stay on the bike. He knew it was all worth it, as long as Fernando was leading them back to Jewel and Blu.

Fernando, Linda, and Tulio sped through the crowd on their motorcycle.

After a few bumps and close calls, Fernando stopped the bike in a dark alley and hopped off.

Linda and Tulio were both dizzy from the ride through the city—and they both had hair sticking out in every direction from the wind. But Fernando seemed fine—he was used to getting around quickly and the commotion of the city never bothered him.

"This way," Fernando said, motioning for Linda and Tulio to follow.

Linda and Tulio were a little unstable on their feet, but they hurried to keep up with Fernando. He showed them a broken part of the wall, covered in corrugated aluminum.

"Through here," he said.

Inside was Marcel's warehouse, where all the smuggled birds were usually kept, except . . . the warehouse was empty!

"What?" Fernando whispered. "But . . . the birds were here! Just yesterday!"

"Sure they were, kid," said Tulio with a sigh.

"I swear!" Fernando insisted. "The birds were right here."

"Well, how do you know?" Linda asked.

"Because . . ." Fernando hesitated. But then he took a deep breath and continued. "Because I'm the one who took them in the first place."

Linda looked shocked and angry. "You took my bird!?"

"I didn't want to hurt anybody. I just . . . I just needed money!"

"But Fernando, I trusted you!" Linda cried.

"I know, but—"

Just then they heard keys in the front door, and the handle started to turn.

Who came through the door was not who Fernando expected. It was Tipa and Armando, dressed in silly Carnavale costumes. They looked around but all they saw was Fernando. That's because Linda and Tulio hid as soon as they heard the door.

"Hey, guys," said Fernando.

Armando looked at him suspiciously. "What are you doing here?"

"I just wanted to see if you had any work for me. . . ," Fernando said.

"Well," said Tipa, "if you were here two hours ago, you could have helped us load the—"

Before Tipa could finish his sentence, Armando elbowed him in the belly.

"Ow! What?" Tipa said.

"Shut up!" said Armando.

"So . . ." Fernando pointed at their costumes. "You guys are dressed for Carnavale?"

"Uh, yeah," Tipa said. "So no one will

notice us when we smuggle these birds—"

Armando elbowed him in the belly again and told him to shut up.

Tipa leaned in closer to Fernando and whispered, "We made a float."

"You made a float?!" Fernando said, extra loudly so Linda and Tulio would be able to hear him from their hiding spot. "Can I come along to the parade? I am a great dancer!"

"Oh, can he come? Pleeease?" Tipa said to Armando.

"Fine, but we gotta hurry," Armando said. "Oh, and I almost forgot." He pointed to Tipa, who started digging around near some empty boxes and crates.

Just behind those boxes, Linda and Tulio were crouched down, hiding!

Tipa sifted around the boxes and Linda and Tulio held their breath, hoping he wouldn't see them. . . .

"Where's the other one?" Tipa muttered. Finally he found what he was looking for— another Carnavale mask, for Fernando to wear.

As Tipa picked up the mask, he turned to

Armando. "Hey, can Fernando join us on the plane too?"

Armando elbowed Tipa in the ribs and told him to shut up as they headed out of the warehouse.

Linda and Tulio breathed a sigh of relief that they hadn't been caught.

After Tipa, Armando, and Fernando left, Linda and Tulio burst out from behind the boxes.

"Come on!" said Tulio. "We can't let them get on the plane!"

Linda and Tulio slipped out of the warehouse and into the street. They ran back to the motorcycle, and Tulio hopped on to drive.

"Um, you can drive a motorcycle, right?" Linda asked.

"Of course I can! You insult me!" Tulio gunned the motor and the bike leaped forward, right out from underneath them. They fell backward and the bike crashed straight into a wall.

Tulio turned to Linda with a sheepish look on his face. "No, I can't drive a motorcycle."

As Tulio and Linda sat in the alleyway,

trying to figure out what to do next, the bird smugglers were heading for the parade with Fernando in tow, determined to find the missing blue macaws and ship them out of town—tonight.

CHAPTER

16

RIO RIO RIO RIO RIO RIO

Later that same day, Nigel checked out the club and found the place a total mess. There was broken glass and spilled food everywhere.

In a corner, Nigel noticed a tiny bird hiding behind a crate of oranges. He snatched the small bird up in his sharp talons.

"What happened here?" Nigel asked the tiny bird.

"I-I-I-I-I don't—help!" said the tiny bird.

"Hmm," said Nigel. "I wonder . . . when I bite down on your head, will it go 'pop' or will it go 'crunch'?"

The tiny bird struggled to escape Nigel's firm grasp. But it was no use.

"Where are the two blue birds? The ones with the chain," Nigel demanded, squeezing the tiny bird harder.

"They—they escaped! On a trolley!" squeaked the smaller bird.

"Never send a monkey to do a bird's business," Nigel muttered, and tossed the tiny bird to the side. Then he spread his wings and flew away to find that trolley and those pesky—but valuable—macaws.

Meanwhile, the sun was setting over the bay as the trolley carrying Blu and Jewel climbed a hill with beautiful views of the scenery below. Blu inched closer to Jewel on the back of the trolley, but he was sweating so much that it wasn't exactly romantic. He didn't even know a bird could sweat so much—but that's how hot it was in Rio!

Rafael stood with Nico and Pedro on the other end of the trolley, watching Blu and Jewel from a distance.

Rafael turned to Pedro. "Blu needs a

little . . . romantic help," said Rafael. "Come on. Let's help set the mood!"

"Alright," Pedro agreed. "Here we go . . . *This is the samba, the sa-sa-sa-samba!*" Pedro began to rap.

"What kind of mood is *that*?"

Nico stepped in Pedro's way. "I've got this one," he said. "All you gotta do, Pedro, is follow my lead."

Pedro stepped aside as Nico began singing. What he sang was a lovely romantic ballad.

"Now that's more like it!" said Rafael.

Then he flew straight into the trees above the trolley, which were full of flowers. He ruffled his wings and then swooped back down. As he did, lots of petals from the trees started falling all around, like snow. It was pretty and peaceful. At the back of the trolley, Blu and Jewel got more comfortable, looking up at the sky with the petals drifting down around them.

Jewel sighed. "What a beautiful night," she said.

"Yeah, it's perfect for . . ." Blu leaned toward Jewel. He was sort of hoping for a kiss. But he wasn't sure if that's what he really wanted.

Which was why he finished his sentence by saying, ". . . the perfect night for softball! Or tennis. Yeah. Low humidity."

Rafael was watching all of this. And he knew that Blu would be the perfect boyfriend for Jewel, if only he would stop saying such silly things. So he did his best to get Blu's attention.

"Psst!" Rafael whispered.

Blu heard him and turned around, while Jewel was still watching the flower petals falling from the trees.

"What?"

"Just tell her, 'you have nice eyes.' Go on! Do it!" said Rafael.

"Okay," said Blu. "Great idea!"

He turned to Jewel and said, "I have beautiful eyes."

"Uh," Jewel said, turning to look at Blu. "Yeah. Okay, sure. You have nice eyes. I guess."

"No!!!" whispered Rafael. "*Her* eyes. Not your eyes, *her* eyes!"

"Oh," said Blu. He turned to Jewel again. "I . . . uh . . . your eyes. Your eyes are totally great. Not mine. I mean, you know . . . mine are okay. But *yours*. Wow. I bet you can see right through them!"

"Blu!" Rafael whispered, hovering close so Jewel wouldn't hear. "Just tell her how you feel!"

"Jewel," Blu said, trying to muster some courage.

"Yeah?" She turned, and the moonlight shone off her beak.

"When I'm near you, I . . ."

"Uh-huh?"

The music Nico and Pedro were singing was getting louder and more beautiful by the second, as Blu and Jewel leaned closer together. . . .

"I feel like . . . ," Blu said. But then he opened his beak a little, and by accident, one of the falling flower petals got caught in his throat. He started coughing and choking and gagging and hacking.

"Oh, how sweet, you're getting choked up," Jewel said. Then she realized he was actually choking. "Oh! You're choking!" she said. She reached around Blu and gave him the Heimlich maneuver so he could breathe again.

Blu coughed up the petal. "Thank you!" he said. But as the trolley came to a stop, he knew that he had ruined the romantic moment between them.

CHAPTER

"Ladies and gentlemen," Rafael announced, "I give you Luiz's garage!"

Finally, Blu and Jewel had arrived! They looked around at the car repair shop. There were several broken-down cars and trucks out front, surrounded by a chain-link fence.

Nico and Pedro flew down to stand next to them. Then they all flew over the fence, leaving Blu and Jewel stuck on the outside.

"After you," Blu said, trying to sound polite.

"No, no, no, no, you first . . . ," said Jewel.

"Oh, please, I insist."

"Okay," Jewel said, attempting to go ahead, but then Blu tried at the same time and they bumped into each other.

For the first time, Blu felt shy around Jewel. And she seemed to feel shy too.

"Guess this is it," Jewel said, looking around at the auto-repair shop. Luiz would cut their chain, and they'd be free of each other.

"Yeah. We had quite an adventure," said Blu.

"I guess things like this don't happen in Tiny Soda."

"Tiny Soda?" Blu asked. Then he laughed. "Oh, you mean Minnesota! That's very good. That's pretty funny, actually." Blu and Jewel started to giggle.

Meanwhile, Rafael was inside, trying to find Luiz.

"Luiz! Buddy—are you here? Hey, I got some friends I want you to meet!"

All of a sudden, a huge bulldog leaped out of one of the cars and charged right at the birds! He was barking and snapping wildly. All the birds, except Blu and Jewel, scattered out of the way and flew to the top of the fence.

Since they couldn't fly, Blu and Jewel scampered toward the gate, trying to get away from the angry bulldog.

But they couldn't run fast enough. The dog caught up and knocked into them, sending them sprawling. Blu and Jewel lay in a heap, feeling dazed. The dog stood over them, drooling. Then, suddenly, the dog started laughing.

"Ahhh, I got yous good!" the dog said, laughing more.

"What?!" cried Blu and Jewel.

"I coulda ripped your throats out! I didn't, but I coulda!" The dog wiped some of the drool off of his face proudly.

Just then, Rafael flew over to them. "Hey, Luiz," he said. "Stop scaring my friends!"

Jewel and Blu looked at each other. *This was Luiz?!?*

"Hey, Rafi!" cried Luiz. "C'mere! Where you been? Lookin' good, man!"

At the same time, Jewel shouted, "Luiz is a bulldog?"

Luiz was a bit offended. "Yous got something against dogs?"

"I do when they're drooling on me!"

Luiz got a hurt look on his face. "It's a medical condition," he said.

Rafael chimed in. "Hey amigo, we really need you."

Luiz pointed at Jewel. "She's mean, bro."

Rafael tried to calm the dog down and make him feel better. "Luiz, come on, please? We need your help!" He showed Luiz the chain that was tying Jewel and Blu together by their ankles.

Luiz studied the chain for a second, and then he said, "I think I know what to do."

He brought the birds over to a machine table that had a large, round saw blade.

Blu, of course, got nervous just seeing that big saw. "Uhhh . . . are you sure this is safe?" he asked.

"Oh sure," said Luiz. "There's nothing to it." Then he tilted his head down and put a mask over his eyes. "If something goes wrong, scream really loud, because I can't hear too good with this mask on. Hey Rafi, get the switch please!"

Rafael could see that Jewel and Blu were uncomfortable. "Don't worry, he's a professional." Then he flipped the switch, and the saw started spinning, showing its sharp teeth and making a high-pitched whining sound.

Luiz nudged Jewel and Blu toward the saw, but they tried to flap the other way. That thing could kill them!

"Try not to move so much," Luiz told them. "I can't really see out of this mask either." Then he pushed them closer to the blade and held them down. But then he slipped in a puddle of his own drool and accidentally shoved Blu and Jewel toward the sharp saw. Blu screamed— his beak was right next to the saw!

Just then Jewel flew up and grabbed onto a hanging light. A feather got clipped off of Blu's head as he was yanked along with Jewel, just in time. Then, the chain made them swing around in the air like a wild pendulum, knocking Luiz straight into the saw, which cut right through his mask! The birds swung back around in the other direction, headed right for Luiz, who started screaming. As the birds crashed into Luiz, the chain caught in his mouth and they all fell over.

Then, something peculiar happened. A big pile of Luiz's drool ran onto the leg cuffs around Jewel and Blu's ankles. Suddenly, the cuffs came undone and Blu and Jewel's legs popped out. They were free! Covered in drool, but free!

"Ewww, gross!" Blu said, trying to wipe the drool off himself. "But I'm free! Jewel, Jewel, we're free! Sticky! But free! Contaminated with germs, probably, but free! Can you believe it's finally—"

Then Blu noticed that Jewel was not listening to him. She was soaring, ecstatically, into the air.

Blu had never seen Jewel so happy. She swirled through the air, and to Blu, it was the most beautiful thing he'd ever seen.

"Come on, guys!" Jewel cried with joy. "Let's go! Yeah!"

Pedro looked at Nico with a smile across his beak. "Yeah, what are we waiting for! Let's go!"

"Yeah, baby!" shouted Nico.

Pretty soon all the birds were flying through the air and singing a great song, with Nico and Pedro doing backup.

But down on the ground, Blu stood watching

them. He still could not fly. And for the first time in his life, he longed to be a part of what they had. That freedom. That fun.

Luiz sat beside Blu. "Yup, I know just how you feel," he said. "It's hard to be stuck down here, just watching those birds. Makes you wanna chase them, and grab 'em in your mouth and bite their heads off, huh!" he said. Then he laughed. "Just kidding, bro! But chasing 'em is plenty fun."

Luiz chuckled as he walked back into the shop, leaving Blu alone, staring at the other birds. Then Blu sighed. He didn't belong here. He just wasn't like these other birds.

With his head hanging low, Blu went to go find the next trolley.

"Hey, where are you going?" Jewel called. "Blu? Blu! What's wrong?"

"Nothing," said Blu. "Everything's perfect. You'll be off to the rain forest, I'll be back with Linda, just like we planned."

Jewel stared at Blu, disappointed. "I guess I thought, maybe . . ."

"What?" said Blu. "That you'd come to Minnesota? Great, I guess I'll knit you a scarf."

"No, that's not what I meant."

Nico, Pedro, and Rafael fluttered down to land near Jewel and Blu and find out what they were talking about.

"Look, Jewel," Blu sighed. "I can't spend my whole life walking around, following you wherever you're going!"

"Hey, it's not my fault you can't fly!"

Nico and Pedro gasped. They were surprised at how harsh Jewel's comment was.

Rafael felt terrible that Blu and Jewel were fighting. "Okay, okay, you know what?" he said. "This is good. Yeah, just clear the air, just be honest with each other."

"You want honesty?" asked Blu. "Fine, I can be honest. I don't belong here. In fact, I never wanted to come here in the first place. And, and, and you know what? I don't even like samba music!"

Nico burst into tears.

"Hey," Pedro shouted at Blu. "Now you've gone too far!"

Blu faced Pedro. "Yeah, I said it! Every song sounds exactly the same! *Tico taco, ya ya ya, Tico, taco, ya ya ya.* Well I'll tell you what, I'm gonna *tico tico* outta here."

"Fine!" Jewel said. "See you around, *pet*." She flew away. Nico and Pedro fluttered after her.

"No!" Rafael cried. "Wait, wait, wait! Come back! You belong together—like Romeo and Juliet!"

But it was no use. Jewel had already disappeared into the distance, with Nico and Pedro close behind. "Oh, young love," Rafael sighed. "Always so melodramatic. Wait, Blu, come back here!"

But Blu was sauntering off. He needed to be alone. Rafael went after him.

Luiz came bounding back out of the shop. He was dressed in a crazy Carnavale costume, with a big funny basket of fruit attached to his head. "Who wants a ride in my fruit?" he called, drool sloshing everywhere as he ran. "Hey, where'd everyone go?"

CHAPTER

18

Meanwhile, Jewel was flying as fast as she could toward the mountains. She was still furious with Blu.

"Jewels! Jewels!" cried Pedro.

"Wait for us!" hollered Nico, close behind.

But Jewel didn't hear them. She was going too fast. And she was crying. A tear slid down her face.

And then, all of a sudden, something swooped down out of the sky, over her. It was Nigel. He grabbed Jewel in his talons.

"Going somewhere, pretty bird?" Nigel asked.

"Oh yeah, I was just on my way to *claw your eyes out*!" Jewel screamed. She tried to claw at Nigel but he was too strong. "Let go of me!"

"Temper, temper," Nigel scolded. "Now come along, my dear. We're going to a parade! Everyone loves a parade." He smirked his evil smirk, and swiftly carried Jewel in the direction of the bright lights of Rio, where Carnavale was in full swing.

"Jewel!" Nico shouted, terrified. But it was too late.

Nico looked at Pedro, who nodded his head. "Nobody messes with a friend of Pedro!" he said. "It's on!"

Nico was a bit scared. "Did you see the talons on that guy?"

Pedro nodded. "You're right. We need help." He started flying back toward the auto shop. "Rafi! Rafi! Help us out! Need a little help!"

Nico fluttered just behind him. "Help! Help!" he called.

As they got closer to Blu, Rafael, and Luiz,

Pedro started shouting, "Blu! Blu! Some crazy white cockatoo got Jewels!"

Blu was stunned. But then a look of determination fell across his face. "Let's fly!" he shouted.

A few seconds later, Blu was inside the fruit basket on top of Luiz's head as wind blew through his feathers. Luiz started running. "Whoo-hooo! Outta my way, people!"

And they were off, determined to save Jewel.

CHAPTER

19

Tipa and Armando were on their way to meet Marcel at the Sambadrome, the place where the big parade was taking place. Marcel had sent them to create a magnificent float to enter into the Carnavale parade. This float would be their disguise, and they would use it to sneak the stolen birds away and sell them.

Marcel was eagerly awaiting their arrival, pacing the street outside the Sambadrome, getting more and more concerned with every minute that Tipa and Armando were late. Then he looked up and saw a beautiful float with a phoenix on it. Marcel clapped his hands together. It was perfect! But then the float passed by. And behind it, Marcel saw Tipa and Armando . . . with a small, sad, ugly float. It looked like a dead chicken. What a disaster! Tipa and Armando were dressed like chickens, too, and Fernando was dressed up as an egg. It looked ridiculous.

Oh well, there was no more time to delay. They'd have to use the ugly little float.

Marcel boarded the float and they headed off to join the parade.

Meanwhile, on the other side of town, Linda and Tulio were back on the motorcycle—this time Linda was driving.

"Excuse me!" Linda shouted, swerving just in time to avoid knocking over a bunch of partiers.

They got to a fence outside of the parade, but a policeman stopped them. "Sorry, folks," he said. "You can only go in there if you're one of the Carnavale performers."

Linda and Tulio hopped back on the bike and rode farther along, looking for a way to

121

sneak into the parade.

Finally they got an idea. They would have to pretend to be performers!

They found a truck full of costumes, and decided to put some on. Tulio discovered a tight blue outfit covered in feathers.

"Wow . . . *Cyanopsitta spixii*!" Tulio ran around pretending to be the bird, talking in his crazy bird language.

Just then, Linda walked out in her own costume and laughed at Tulio. Tulio stopped running around and squawking, embarrassed.

Linda was dressed in a bird costume too. She looked silly, but Tulio thought she was beautiful. In fact, they looked a lot like Blu and Jewel! Fireworks went off in the distance as Tulio stepped closer to Linda. She looked so pretty covered in all those bright feathers, he almost wanted to kiss her. . . .

But as Tulio got closer to Linda, their costume beaks crashed into each other.

"Oh, sorry!" Linda said, moving out of the way.

Tulio smiled. "Come with me," he said. He took her hand and they ran toward the line of performers waiting to enter into the parade. The guard saw Linda with Tulio and assumed they were both performers, too, so he let them pass.

"Just follow my lead," Tulio whispered to Linda.

As soon as they stepped into the crowd of people dressed in colorful costumes, they started calling out for Blu.

Then a Carnavale producer in a yellow jacket spotted Linda. He didn't speak English so he was shouting to her in Portuguese, the language of Brazil.

Linda didn't understand what he was saying, but clearly he was trying to tell her something. He grabbed her arm and pulled her away while Tulio wasn't looking.

"Wait! Where are you taking me?" Linda cried. "Tulio? Tulio, help!"

But the producer thought that Linda was the star of the garden float! So he shoved her inside a dark float as Linda shouted and pounded on the closed door. It was very dark and Linda couldn't really tell where she was.

That is, until the walls of the float started

to peel down around her. They were giant fake flower petals. And Linda was at the center. Now she could see that crowds and crowds of people were surrounding the float, waiting for the performers to sing and dance. And Linda was center stage. They expected *her* to perform!

"Well, cheese and crackers!" Linda exclaimed, not sure what to do, but feeling pretty embarrassed.

Finally, she spotted Tulio in the crowd. Just then the producer started shouting at her, *"Rebola! Rebola!"*

"What does he mean?" Linda shouted toward Tulio.

Tulio got a funny look on his face. "He said he wants you to, you know . . . shake your butt!"

"Oh, dear!" Linda muttered. But since everyone was watching her, she figured she better do something. So slowly, nervously, she started to dance.

At the same time, Blu was just arriving at the parade, still riding the fruit basket attached to

Luiz's costume, with Rafael, Nico, and Pedro flying overhead. As they scanned the crowd, Blu saw Linda on top of the garden float. She was dancing!

At the same time, Linda saw Blu. "Blu?!" she shouted.

"Linda?!" he squawked.

But as much as he wanted to go straight to Linda, he had to save Jewel first!

"Let's go get Jewel!" he squawked, then held on tight to Luiz's head as Luiz charged through the crowd toward the chicken float.

But Luiz was having a hard time making his way through the chaos, and the tail of someone's costume knocked Blu off Luiz's back. He looked around for a way to keep going, and saw a skateboard. He jumped onto it and zipped through the crowd, shouting, "Comin' through! Watch it!"

Finally he got to the chicken float. Inside it, Jewel was sitting there in a cage, all alone.

"Blu!" she cried. "You shouldn't have come!"

Just then, Nigel entered the float and captured Blu, putting him in another cage. *That's okay*, Blu thought. *My friends will save me. Right?*

But then Blu looked around, and he saw that Rafael, Nico, and Pedro were all caught in cages too. Oh, no!

CHAPTER

By then, Linda had climbed down from the garden float. She and Tulio looked around frantically to see where Blu had gone. Just then, Sylvio ran up to them.

"I saw them!" he said. "They went that way!"

Linda and Tulio ran after the chicken float, but it was just about to exit the parade route—they would have to hurry if they were going to rescue Blu.

Linda saw a driver getting out of his float, and she had an idea. She hopped into the float and started following the smugglers in their float.

The chicken float was hard to follow, but Fernando, still in his egg costume, stood at the edge of it, kicking little pieces of the float off. Linda saw what Fernando was doing. She followed the chunks of glued feathers as they wafted past, and she was able to keep track of where the ugly chicken float was, with the evil bird smugglers inside.

Tulio hopped into Linda's float and they took off after the smugglers.

As soon as they got to an abandoned airport, the smugglers started unloading the float and putting cages full of stolen birds onto one of the planes.

Fernando found Blu's cage and opened the door. "You're free now," Fernando whispered to Blu. "Go! Quickly!"

But Nigel swooped and closed the cage again, just as Marcel walked over. "What are you doing, boy?" Marcel demanded.

"N-n-nothing . . ."

Then Marcel looked up and saw the float

that Linda and Tulio were driving. He also saw the trail Fernando had left for them.

Marcel grabbed Fernando's arm. "You shouldn't have done that!" he shouted, dragging Fernando toward the plane. Fernando bit Marcel's hand, and when Marcel let go, screaming in pain, Fernando ran.

"Just forget him!" Marcel shouted. "Let's go."

He got onto the plane with the cages of birds, including the cages containing Blu and Jewel.

"We're too late!" Tulio cried, leaping off of the float and running toward the plane.

"We'll see about that!" Linda said as the plane started to lift off the ground.

CHAPTER

21

Inside the cargo hold of the plane, the birds were getting worried again. This did *not* look good.

"Sorry, Eva," Rafael muttered to himself, "but it looks like I won't be home for dinner!"

Blu had an idea. He tried the lock on his cage, but he couldn't get it open. Then something caught his eye—it was a bungee cord and it was dangling from the ceiling just above his cage. He grabbed it and stretched it tight before hooking it onto the bars of his cage.

"What are you doing?" Jewel asked.

"I'm going to get us out of here," Blu said.

When Blu bit through the cord connecting his cage to all the other cages, the bungee swung his cage into the wall and the cage broke open. He was free!

Right away he went around unlocking everyone's cages, starting with Jewel's. Nico, Pedro, and Rafael helped him out by breaking some of the cages open.

Then Blu flipped the wire switch that opened the cargo hatch. It set off an alarm that could be heard in the cockpit.

"What the . . . !" shouted Marcel, hearing the alarm. He looked over and saw the cargo hatch wobbling like the door was about to open. He grabbed the door handle and tried to force the door open, but the fallen cages were blocking the door.

Meanwhile, inside the cargo hold all the birds were running for the hatch. Some jumped out the back of the plane and soared high into the sky, finally free.

Just then, Marcel managed to open the door a crack, and Nigel flew through it and leaped on top of Blu, digging his talons into Blu's neck.

"Let him go!" Jewel gasped, jumping onto Nigel's back.

Nigel swatted her off of him and she slammed into the wall of the plane.

"Ow! My wing!" she cried. She wasn't sure if she could fly with it—it felt broken.

But then Blu saw a cargo strap dangling in the wind. He grabbed it and tied it around Nigel's feet, then gave Nigel a firm kick in the chest.

Nigel hit the cargo door, and it burst open. Nigel went flying out, and got sucked straight into the engine of the plane with a loud *THUMP-THUMP-THUMP-HISSSS*. Soon, white feathers were floating all over the plane.

But then, the engine sputtered to a stop. And the plane started falling. . . .

Tipa, Armando, and Marcel all grabbed parachutes and jumped overboard.

"Blu! Help!" Jewel called out as she slid toward the edge of the open hatch.

"Nooo!" shouted Blu as he watched her fall. He stood on the edge of the door, terrified, feeling the wind rush through his feathers. He had no choice. It was now or never.

He had to fly.

And so he jumped out of the plane. And spread his wings. And tumbled through the air, determined to save Jewel.

Down on the tarmac, Linda was sitting with her head in her hands.

She didn't see Blu and Jewel falling through the sky.

In the air, Blu caught up with Jewel, turned, and kissed her. He had no choice. He had to save her. He grabbed her and started to fly, helping Jewel toward safety.

Fernando reached over and tapped Linda on the shoulder. He pointed to the two birds and said, "Look!"

"It's Blu!" Linda said, leaping to her feet with joy. "He's flying!"

Blu spotted Linda and swooped down, carrying Jewel gently. He set her down and Tulio rushed over. He noticed immediately that her wing was hurt.

"Don't worry," Tulio said, "I'll take care of her."

CHAPTER

22

A few months later...

Tulio nursed Jewel back to health, and now she was strong enough to fly again on her own. He brought her back into the rain forest and set her free. Tulio had hired Fernando to be his assistant, and together they had created a special area in the forest, a bird sanctuary. No one smuggled birds out of this part of the forest. All the birds that lived here were safe.

As soon as Tulio let go, Jewel soared into the sky, swirling through the leaves of the trees, flying and singing to her heart's delight.

Blu and Linda watched her from the forest

floor. Blu turned to face Linda, and they did a fist bump. Then Blu took off after Jewel—flying right beside her. He even did a few flips just to impress her.

Then, from beyond the trees, a bunch of baby macaws started squawking. "Mom! Dad!" they cried. "Wait up!"

Pretty soon, a whole group of adorable blue macaw chicks came flitting and dancing along, following Blu and Jewel. They were Blu and Jewel's children!

As they all flew around, they were joined by Nico and Pedro and Kipo. Just then, Rafael popped out of his nest and hollered after them. "Wait for me too!"

Rafael started singing, and pretty soon Eva heard him and came out. She started singing with him, but her voice was so horrible that all the other birds in the forest immediately stopped their song. Someone tried to throw a piece of fruit at her!

"Ah, my love," said Rafael to his wife, "your singing is kind of an acquired taste." With that, Eva stopped singing, and the rest of the birds went back to their song and dance.

Tulio was so excited to see all of these wild birds in their natural habitat, celebrating and singing their samba songs. He tried to talk to them in their language, shouting, "Squaw-kaw! Squaw-kaw!" and flapping his arms.

The baby macaws rolled their eyes. "That guy's crazy!" they whispered to each other.

Linda came over to Tulio and smiled at him. Then she held his hand and they watched the birds.

The baby macaws followed Blu and Jewel and the whole happy family flew off into the setting sun.